D1144081

This Walker book
belongs to:

_____

For Mum

First published 2009 by Walker Books Ltd
87 Vauxhall Walk, London SE11 5HJ

This edition published 2012

2 4 6 8 10 9 7 5 3 1

This book has been typeset in Gill Sans MT Schoolbook

Printed in China

British Library Cataloguing in Publication Data:
a catalogue record for this book is available
from the British Library

ISBN 978-1-4063-4049-5

www.walker.co.uk

Tilly and
her friends
all live
together in
a little yellow
house...

Pretty
Pru

Polly Dunbar

WALKER BOOKS
AND SUBSIDIARIES
LONDON • BOSTON • SYDNEY • AUCKLAND

"Oh pretty,"
said Pru,
"I'm so pretty!"

She was
putting on her
favourite
red lipstick.

"Can I have some make-up?" said Tumpty.

"Then I can be pretty like you."

"No,"
said Pru.
"You'll
waste it."

"Humpf," said Tumpty.

So while Pru

was busy doing

a pretty-

prance ...

Tumpty stretched out his very
long trunk and took Pru's handbag!

"Look, everybody," said Tumpty.

"Now we can be pretty like Pru."

"Tilly, **Tilly, Tilly,**"
Pru called.
"My handbag,
it's lost."

"Don't worry," said Tilly.

"It can't be far away."

"Hello, Hector,"
said Tilly.
"Pru's lost
her handbag.
Do you
have it?"

"No," said Hector.

"My handbag!"
cried Pru,
"my green
handbag
with red
spots.

Tiptoe,
have you seen it?"

Tiptoe blushed
the prettiest shade of pink.

"Doodle!"
flapped Pru.
"Have **you**
seen my
handbag ...

with my blusher
and nail varnish?"

"It wasn't me!" said Doodle,
and she pointed a very pretty finger.

She was
pointing at
Tumpty.

Tumpty was doing
a pretty-prance
of his own.

He looked **extremely funny.**

Everybody laughed ...

everybody except Pru.

"That's **my handbag** on your head," said Pru.

Everybody

stopped laughing.

"I'm sorry,"

Tumpty said.

With a curl of his very long trunk,

he gave Pru her handbag back.

"We're
sorry too,"
said
Hector.

And they put the make-up back in the bag.

Then Pru did
something very special.
She gave Tumpty
her **favourite** red lipstick.

Tumpty did something
very special too...

He let

everybody

have a go ...

and they all pranced prettily,

just like Pru.

The End

Polly Dunbar

Polly Dunbar is one of today's most exciting young author-illustrators,
her warm and witty books captivating children the world over.

Polly based the Tilly and Friends stories on her own experience of
sharing a house with friends. Tilly, Hector, Tumpty, Doodle, Tiptoe and Pru
are all very different and they don't always get on. But in the little yellow
house, full of love and laughter, no one can be sad or cross for long!

ISBN 978-1-4063-4024-2

ISBN 978-1-4063-4048-8

ISBN 978-1-4063-4049-5

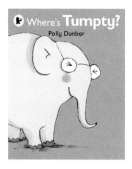

ISBN 978-1-4063-4045-7

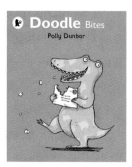

ISBN 978-1-4063-4046-4

ISBN 978-1-4063-4047-1

"Nobody can draw anything more instantly loveable than one of Dunbar's characters."
Independent on Sunday

Available from all good booksellers

www.walker.co.uk